TREASURY OF

BEDTIME STORIES

Adapted by
Jane Jerrard
Bette Killion
Carolyn Quattrocki

Illustrated by
Tim Ellis
Burgandy Nilles
Jim Salvati
Susan Spellman

Cover illustrated by
Wendy Edelson

PUBLICATIONS INTERNATIONAL, LTD.

Louis Weber, C.E.O.
Publications International, Ltd.
7373 North Cicero Avenue
Lincolnwood, Illinois 60646

Manufactured in the U.S.A.

8 7 6 5 4 3 2 1

ISBN: 0-7853-1356-7

CONTENTS

GOLDILOCKS
and the
THREE BEARS

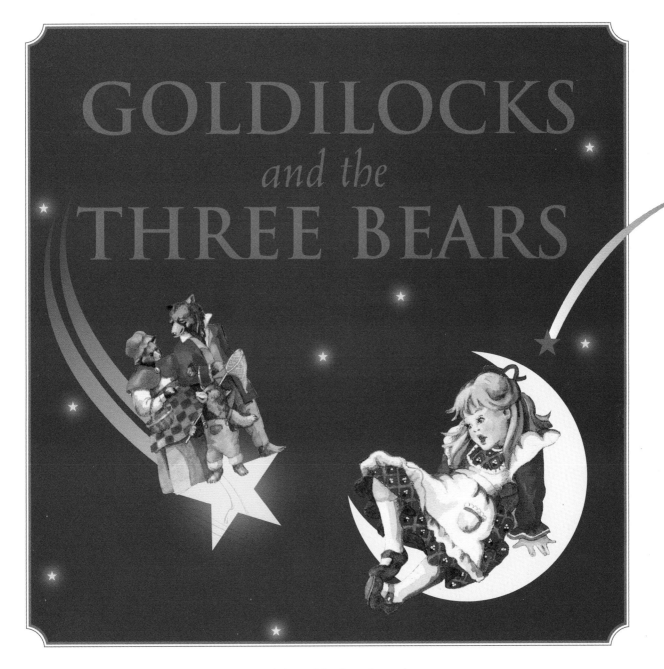

Adapted by Jane Jerrard

Illustrated by Burgandy Nilles

There once was a family of three bears. There was a great big Papa Bear, a middle-size Mama Bear, and a wee little Baby Bear. The three bears lived in a cozy little house right in the middle of the forest.

The three bears always started each day in the very same way. First they washed their faces and paws with sparkling fresh water and sweet-smelling soap. Then they made their beds and fluffed their feather pillows. After they were dressed for the day, they went downstairs for a nice breakfast of delicious porridge.

One bright morning Mama Bear cooked the porridge and called her family for breakfast, just as she did every day, rain or shine. She spooned the porridge into their three bowls, and they all sat down to eat.

"It's too hot!" exclaimed Baby Bear, tasting the porridge in his wee little bowl.

"We must let the porridge cool for a little while," agreed Papa Bear and Mama Bear, after they tasted the porridge in their bowls.

The three bears decided to go for a walk while their hot breakfast cooled. Mama Bear took her basket in case they happened to find ripe blackberries to put on top of their porridge.

Now it just so happened that a little girl named Goldilocks was out walking in the woods that morning, all by herself.

She had been walking since quite early and was feeling rather tired. She was hungry as well, because she had left her house without eating breakfast. When Goldilocks saw the bears' little house, she thought it was the perfect place to rest.

Goldilocks marched up to the front door and knocked, but there was no answer. The bears were still out taking their walk. So Goldilocks just let herself in!

Goldilocks saw the three bowls of porridge. Her mouth started to water and her stomach started to rumble at once. She decided that she simply must taste the porridge.

First she dipped the spoon into the great big bowl that belonged to Papa Bear. "Ooo, this porridge is too hot!" she cried.

Next she tried the middle-size bowl that belonged to Mama Bear. "This porridge is too cold!" she said.

Last she had a taste from the wee little bowl that belonged to Baby Bear. "This porridge is just right!" she said, and she gobbled it all up.

After she had eaten the porridge, Goldilocks wanted to rest. She went into the bears' sitting room, where she saw three chairs.

First she sat down in the great big chair. "This chair is too hard!" she said.

Next she tried the middle-size chair. "This chair is too soft!" she said, struggling to get out.

Last she tried the wee little chair that was just the right size for her to sit in. "This chair is just right!" she smiled. But Goldilocks sat down so hard that the wee little chair broke all to pieces!

By this time Goldilocks was very sleepy. She tiptoed up the stairs and found three beds.

First she lay down on the great big bed. "This bed is too high at the head!" she said.

Next she tried the middle-size bed. "This bed is too high at the foot!" she frowned.

Last Goldilocks lay down on Baby Bear's wee little bed. And she said, "This bed is just right!" Soon Goldilocks fell fast asleep.

A short time later the three bears returned home from their walk. They noticed right away that things were not quite right.

Papa Bear looked at his great big bowl of porridge and said in his great big voice, "Someone has been eating my porridge!"

Mama Bear looked at her middle-size bowl of porridge and said in her middle-size voice, "Someone has been eating my porridge!"

Baby Bear looked at his wee little bowl and said in his wee little voice, "Someone has been eating my porridge AND HAS EATEN IT ALL UP!"

The three bears then went into their sitting room. When he saw his great big chair, Papa Bear said in his great big voice, "Someone has been sitting in my chair!"

Mama Bear looked at her middle-size chair and said in her middle-size voice, "Someone has been sitting in my chair!"

Baby Bear looked at his wee little chair and cried in his wee little voice, "Someone has been sitting in my chair AND HAS BROKEN IT ALL TO PIECES!"

The three bears went up the stairs to their bedroom. Papa Bear looked at his great big bed and said in his great big voice, "Someone has been sleeping in my bed!"

When Mama Bear looked at her middle-size bed, she said in her middle-size voice, "Someone has been sleeping in my bed!"

Baby Bear looked at his wee little bed and cried in his wee little voice, "Someone has been sleeping in my bed, AND THERE SHE IS!"

Baby Bear's wee little voice woke Goldilocks. She sat up to find three bears staring at her. They did not look pleased to see her!

Quick as a wink, she rolled out of bed and ran straight to the window. She jumped right out and ran off as fast as her legs would carry her.

The three bears never saw Goldilocks again.

HANSEL
and
GRETEL

Adapted by Jane Jerrard

Illustrated by Susan Spellman

Long ago a woodcutter lived on the edge of a large forest with his two children and his wife who was the children's stepmother. The woodcutter's son was called Hansel and his daughter, Gretel. Although the woodcutter worked hard, he was very poor. One year there was a terrible famine in the land. The woodcutter did not have enough food for his family.

The woodcutter's wife complained that the whole family would soon die of hunger. So one night she told her husband that he must take the children deep into the woods and leave them there.

Hansel heard them talking and told Gretel about their stepmother's idea. The children were both very frightened. Then Hansel made a plan.

Later that night, when his parents were sleeping and the moon was high, the boy sneaked outside and gathered as many white pebbles as his pockets would hold.

The next morning the stepmother told Hansel and Gretel that they were all going to gather firewood. As they walked deeper and deeper into the woods, Hansel would stop now and then to look toward his house. Hansel was scolded by his stepmother for being slow, but he was really dropping the white pebbles to mark the way home.

When they finally stopped, the woodcutter built a fire and left the children some crusts of bread for their supper. He said he and his wife would return when they were done cutting wood. Hansel and Gretel knew that they would not be back. They slept for a while by the fire, waiting for nightfall. Then, with the moonlight shining on the white pebbles, Hansel and Gretel followed the trail straight back to their home.

"You bad children!" cried the stepmother when she saw Hansel and Gretel. "Why did you sleep so long?" But she was secretly angry that they had returned.

The next day the woman made her husband lead Hansel and Gretel back into the woods.

This time the woodcutter led Hansel and Gretel deeper into the forest. Hansel had not had time to gather pebbles, so he crumbled his bread and left a trail of crumbs instead. Hansel and Gretel slept until the moon rose, then they searched for the path of breadcrumbs. But the bread had been eaten by the birds in the forest, so they could not find their way home.

They searched until they were so tired that they had to stop and sleep. The next morning they searched again. Then Hansel and Gretel saw a beautiful white bird who sang so sweetly they followed him as he flew from branch to branch.

Soon they found themselves in a small field where they saw the most amazing house. It was made of gingerbread, with a roof of icing and windows made of sugar!

The children were so hungry they didn't stop to think. They each broke off a piece of the house and started to eat it. No sooner had they stuffed their mouths than they heard a gentle voice calling:

Nibble, nibble like a mouse,
Who's that nibbling at my house?

The door of the house opened, and there stood an old woman leaning on a heavy cane. Hansel and Gretel were so frightened that they dropped what they were eating.

The woman smiled and invited Hansel and Gretel into her house. Seeing how hungry and tired they were, she gave them a wonderful dinner of pancakes and apples. Then she made up beds for them and put them right to sleep, as kind as any grandmother.

Hansel and Gretel did not know that the woman who seemed so nice was really a wicked witch!

Before Hansel and Gretel awoke the next morning, the witch carried Hansel to a little cage that she had built and locked him inside.

⁓

"Now," she cackled, "I'll fatten him up. He'll make a tasty treat for me to eat!"

Then she woke poor Gretel and ordered her to fetch water and cook food for Hansel, because she wanted him to grow plump. Hansel and Gretel cried and begged to be set free, but the witch just laughed.

Each day the witch, who could not see very well, wanted to feel Hansel's finger through the bars of his cage. She wanted to know whether he was getting plump enough to eat. But he cleverly gave her only an old bone to feel. She thought he was still much too thin for her to eat!

Four weeks went by, and Hansel didn't seem to grow any fatter. Gretel could see that the witch was becoming very impatient.

One morning the witch ordered Gretel to make a fire. After a while she told Gretel to climb up into the oven to see if the fire was ready. But Gretel said, "How can I get into the oven to see?"

The witch became angry at that and climbed up into the oven to show Gretel how to look at the fire. Quick as a wink, Gretel gave the witch a hard shove that sent her tumbling all the way in. Then she banged the door shut.

Gretel ran to free Hansel. Now that they had nothing to fear, they explored the witch's house. They found boxes of jewels and gold coins in every corner.

～

The children filled their pockets with riches and set out to find their way home. Before they had gone very far, they came to the edge of a wide lake.

"How will we ever cross without a bridge or a boat?" asked Hansel.

"Here comes a swan," answered Gretel. "I will ask her if she can help us."

The good bird agreed to carry them across the lake one at a time. Once on the other side, Hansel and Gretel found themselves in a familiar little wood. Soon they were running down the path for home.

The woodcutter cried tears of joy to see his children once again. He had not had one moment of peace since he had left them in the forest. And his wife had died while they were gone.

Gretel emptied the jewels from her apron into her father's lap. Pearls and rubies scattered onto the floor. Hansel added handfuls of gold from his pockets.

Hansel and Gretel and their father lived happily for the rest of their days, with the help of the witch's gold!

HENNY PENNY

Adapted by Carolyn Quattrocki
Illustrated by Tim Ellis

One fine day Henny Penny was eating corn in the small yard beside her house. The sun was shining, and Henny Penny stood under a large oak tree.

Suddenly boink! An acorn fell out of the tree and hit Henny Penny right on the top of her head.

"Oh my!" she cried. "The sky is falling. I must go and tell the king."

So Henny Penny tied a scarf around her head, and she gathered up a basketful of corn to eat on her journey. Then she set off down the road to tell the king that the sky was falling.

On her way she passed the house of Cocky Locky.
Cocky Locky was working hard, building a new porch.
"Henny Penny, where are you going?" he called.

"Oh Cocky Locky, the sky is falling, and I am going
to tell the king!" said Henny Penny.

"How do you know it is falling?" asked Cocky Locky.

"I saw it with my own eyes and heard it with my own ears, and a piece of it fell on my head!" said Henny Penny.

"Then I will go with you to tell the king," Cocky Locky said to Henny Penny.

Henny Penny and Cocky Locky went along until they met Ducky Lucky. Ducky Lucky was just returning from her morning swim. "Good morning, Henny Penny and Cocky Locky," said Ducky Lucky. "Where are you going?"

"The sky is falling, and we are going to tell the king," said Cocky Locky.

"How do you know the sky is falling?" asked Ducky Lucky.

"Henny Penny told me," said Cocky Locky.

"I saw it with my own eyes and heard it with my own ears, and a piece of it fell on my head!" said Henny Penny.

"Then I will go with both of you to tell the king," said Ducky Lucky.

Henny Penny, Cocky Locky, and Ducky Lucky went along until they met Goosey Loosey. "Good morning, Henny Penny, Cocky Locky, and Ducky Lucky," said Goosey Loosey. "Where are you going?"

"The sky is falling, and we are going to tell the king," said Ducky Lucky.

"How do you know it is falling?" asked Goosey Loosey.

"Cocky Locky told me," said Ducky Lucky.

"Henny Penny told me," said Cocky Locky.

"I saw it with my own eyes and heard it with my own ears, and a piece of it fell on my head!" said Henny Penny.

"Then I'll go with you to tell the king," said Goosey Loosey.

Henny Penny, Cocky Locky, Ducky Lucky, and Goosey Loosey all went along until they met Turkey Lurkey in front of her garden. "Good morning, Henny Penny, Cocky Locky, Ducky Lucky, and Goosey Loosey," said Turkey Lurkey. "Where are all of you going?"

"The sky is falling, and we are going to tell the king," said Goosey Loosey.

"How do you know it is falling?" asked Turkey Lurkey.

"Ducky Lucky told me," said Goosey Loosey.

"Cocky Locky told me," said Ducky Lucky.

"Henny Penny told me," said Cocky Locky.

"I saw it with my own eyes and heard it with my own ears, and a piece of it fell on my head!" said Henny Penny.

"Then I'll go with you to tell the king," said Turkey Lurkey.

They all went along until they met up with Foxy Loxy.

"Good morning," said Foxy Loxy. "Where are you going?"

"The sky is falling, and we are going to tell the king," said Turkey Lurkey.

"How do you know it is falling?" asked Foxy Loxy.

"Goosey Loosey told me," said Turkey Lurkey.

"Ducky Lucky told me," said Goosey Loosey.

"Cocky Locky told me," said Ducky Lucky.

"Henny Penny told me," said Cocky Locky.

"I saw it with my own eyes and heard it with my own ears, and a piece of it fell on my head!" said Henny Penny.

"Then come with me. I will show you a shorter way to the king's palace," said Foxy Loxy.

Henny Penny, Cocky Locky, Ducky Lucky, Goosey Loosey, and Turkey Lurkey said to Foxy Loxy, "Oh yes, please show us the shorter way to the king's palace. We would be very grateful to you because we must hurry to tell him that the sky is falling."

"Just follow me, Henny Penny, Cocky Locky, Ducky Lucky, Goosey Loosey, and Turkey Lurkey," said Foxy Loxy. "We'll go right up this hill and across this bridge and down this road. Before you know it, we'll be at the king's palace. And you can all tell him that the sky is falling!"

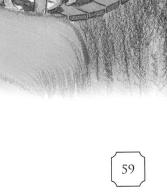

Henny Penny, Cocky Locky, Ducky Lucky, Goosey
Loosey, and Turkey Lurkey all followed Foxy Loxy.

Soon they came to the entrance of a dark cave.
What Henny Penny, Cocky Locky, Ducky Lucky,
Goosey Loosey, and Turkey Lurkey did not know
was that this dark cave was really Foxy Loxy's home!

"Just follow me through here," said Foxy Loxy,
"and we'll soon be at the king's palace."

Cocky Locky, Ducky Lucky, Goosey Loosey, and
Turkey Lurkey all followed Foxy Loxy into the cave.
Henny Penny was last in line, and she was frightened.
She started to run away.

Henny Penny ran and
ran as fast as her legs would
carry her. She ran back along
the long road. She ran across
the narrow bridge. And she
ran down the steep hill.

Henny Penny quickly ran
past Turkey Lurkey's garden.
She ran past the place where
Goosey Loosey had been on

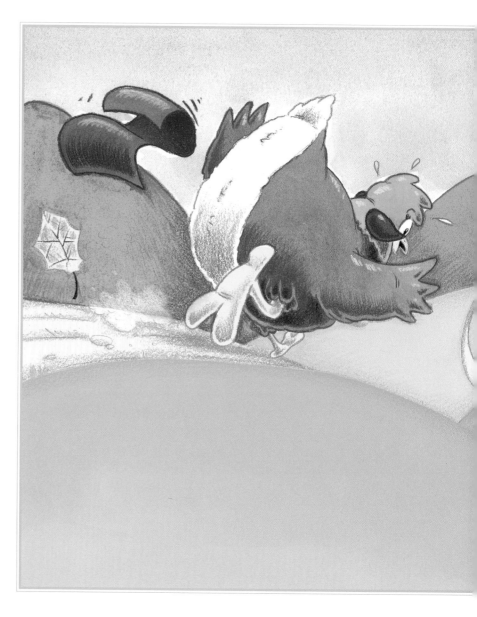

her way to market. She ran
past Ducky Lucky's pond,
and Henny Penny ran past
Cocky Locky's house.

Henny Penny ran and ran
until, up ahead, she saw her
cozy little house with the oak
tree beside it. She could even
see the corn scattered on the
ground underneath the tree.

Henny Penny ran all the way home! She was last seen scratching happily for corn in her little yard. And the king never did hear that the sky was falling.

PUSS
in
BOOTS

Adapted by Jane Jerrard
Illustrated by Susan Spellman

Once upon a time, there was a poor country man who had raised three sons. When the man died, they agreed to divide up the few things he owned. The oldest took his house, the middle son got his donkey, and the youngest son was left with only his father's cat, Puss.

"What on earth will I do with a cat?" moaned the young man. He could barely keep himself fed and had nothing to offer a pet.

Puss overheard the third son and answered, "Don't worry, master. If you give me a sack and a pair of boots, you'll find that you have the most valuable thing your father ever owned."

The youngest son, feeling that he had nothing to lose, gave the cat what he asked for.

The cat put on the old pair of boots and took the sack to a place where he knew many fat rabbits came to find dinner. He put some tender young grass in the sack and lay down beside it as if he were dead. Soon enough, Puss caught a plump, brown rabbit in his sack.

He carried his catch straight to the castle and asked to see the king himself! When Puss was brought before the king, he bowed low and offered the king the nice fat rabbit, saying, "Sire, please accept this gift from my master, the duke of Carabas." (For that is the name he had chosen for his master.)

"Thank your master for me," answered the king.

A few days later the cat returned and gave the king a pair of fat, white doves, and a few days after that, he brought a dozen quail eggs.

For several weeks Puss brought many gifts to the king, explaining that the presents were from the duke of Carabas. The king was charmed by such a well-mannered cat and enjoyed the presents very much.

But he was beginning to wonder about the cat's master. Who was the mysterious duke of Carabas, and why had the king never heard of him? The king finally decided that, whoever he was, the duke was certainly a friendly and generous person.

One day the cat learned that the king and his daughter would be riding near the river. Puss went to his master and told him to take off his shirt and breeches and stand in the river near the bridge at noon the next day.

Trusting Puss, his master did everything he was asked. The next day at noon, as the king's carriage was crossing the bridge, the cat cried out, "Help! Help! My master, the duke of Carabas, is drowning!"

The king knew the cat and the name of the duke well enough, and he ordered his guards to save the man.

Puss told the king that his master's clothes had been stolen from him. The king insisted on dressing the duke of Carabas in an extra suit of his own clothes. The duke was grateful and thanked the king for his kindness. He looked quite handsome in the fine clothes. The king's daughter, who was very beautiful, told him so.

The king invited the duke to ride with his daughter and him. As they rode happily in the carriage, the cat ran ahead of the royal coach, quite pleased with himself.

As he ran ahead of the coach, Puss ordered every farmer and worker he met on the road, "You must tell the king the land you work on belongs to the duke of Carabas. If you do not, the ogre who lives in that far castle will chop you into tiny pieces for stew!"

All the farmers and workers were very frightened of the ogre in the castle, so they all did what the cat asked.

When the king stopped to ask whose land he was crossing, he heard, "the duke of Carabas!" no matter how far he went.

"You certainly do have a lot of land," the king said to the duke.

The princess smiled at him, and the duke smiled back. He had no idea what was happening. He was just thinking how beautiful the princess was.

At last Puss came to the great castle, which really did belong to the ogre, and so did all the lands they had passed through. Puss knew all about the ogre. He went right into the castle and asked to see him.

Soon enough the cat was brought before the ogre.

"It is said that you can take the shape of any animal you choose," said Puss to the ogre, "that you can, if you wish, turn yourself into a lion."

"True enough," said the ogre proudly, and he turned himself into a lion.

The cat, seeing a fierce lion suddenly appear, was so frightened that he jumped onto a tall cupboard. But his boots slipped out from under him, and he slid back down. The ogre had turned back into an ogre again.

Puss admitted that he had been quite frightened and complimented the ogre on his skill.

"People also say that you can change yourself into the tiniest of creatures," said Puss. "A mouse, for example. But that is impossible!"

"Impossible?" cried the ogre. "Watch this!" And he changed himself into a mouse right then and there.

Well of course, Puss, being a cat, gobbled him up in one quick bite!

Just then the king's carriage arrived at the castle gate. Puss ran to meet it, saying, "Welcome, sire, to the castle of the duke of Carabas."

"Why, is this your castle, my friend?" the king asked the duke. "May we come in?"

The duke only smiled and turned to help the princess out of the carriage. At the cat's orders, the ogre's servants prepared a wonderful meal for the guests.

While they ate, it was decided that the princess should marry the duke of Carabas right away, since it was plain that they were in love.

As for Puss in Boots, he became a great lord and never had to hunt for mice again—except sometimes for fun.

JACK
and the
BEANSTALK

Adapted by Jane Jerrard

Illustrated by Susan Spellman

Long ago, there lived a poor woman and her son named Jack. They had no money and no food, so the woman decided that they must sell their milking cow.

The woman asked Jack to take the cow into town and offer her for sale. On the road into town, Jack met a strange man who asked to buy the cow.

"I will give you five magic beans for your cow," he said to Jack. "Do you know how many that is?"

"Two for each of my hands and one in my mouth!" answered Jack.

"Right!" said the strange man. "Here are the beans." So Jack traded the cow for the five magic beans.

When Jack returned home, he proudly told his mother of the good trade he had made.

"You foolish boy!" she said, "now we will go hungry!" And she threw the beans out the window, because she did not believe they were magic. She sent Jack to bed without any supper, even though there was nothing to eat anyway.

The next morning, Jack awoke to find a large beanstalk growing from the spot where the beans had fallen. It was so tall that it grew all the way to the sky!

Jack climbed the beanstalk until he was high in the sky, even higher than the clouds. And there before him he saw a great castle.

Jack walked up to the castle. There in the doorway stood the biggest woman he had ever seen!

"Please, Ma'am, I am very hungry. Could I come in and have something to eat?" asked Jack.

The woman said that her husband, who was a giant, was coming home soon and would eat Jack for supper. But Jack asked again so nicely that the woman brought him inside and gave him some breakfast.

No sooner had Jack finished eating than he heard the tramp, tramp, tramp of the giant's boots.

Quickly, the woman hid Jack in the unlit oven.

The giant filled the kitchen door and roared,

Fe-fi-fo-fum,
I smell the blood of an Englishman!
Be he live or be he dead,
I'll grind his bones to make my bread!

"You only smell the stew I have cooked," said his wife, setting a huge bowl in front of him.

After the giant had eaten his fill, he called for his gold. His wife brought bags of gold coins. The giant counted them until he grew sleepy. Soon he began to snore.

Jack slipped out of the dark oven and grabbed one of the bags of gold. Then he ran as fast as he could to the beanstalk and climbed down.

Jack's mother was happy to have him home, and the gold bought them food for many months. But as soon as the coins were spent, Jack disguised himself and climbed the beanstalk past the clouds. Once again he asked the giant's wife to let him into the castle.

The woman did not recognize Jack in his disguise. But she did not want to let him in. She told Jack that the last boy she had let in for food had stolen a bag of her husband's gold.

But Jack asked so nicely for a drink that she brought him to the kitchen and gave him a thimble of water.

No sooner had Jack finished the water than he heard the tramping of giant boots and ran to hide in the oven. The giant roared,

Fe-fi-fo-fum,
I smell the blood of an Englishman!
Be he live or be he dead,
I'll grind his bones to make my bread!

His wife said, "You only smell the delicious soup I have cooked for you." Then she fed the giant his supper.

After the giant had eaten, he told his wife to bring his magic hen.

"Lay an egg!" commanded the giant. The hen laid a perfect golden egg. Soon the giant fell asleep, and Jack crept out from his hiding place. He grabbed the hen and did not stop running until he was safely home.

Each day the hen laid another golden egg. Jack and his mother were able to sell the eggs to buy plenty of food. Jack's mother was very happy.

But Jack still longed for adventure. So he climbed up the beanstalk once more and tiptoed into the giant's castle. He ran into the kitchen and hid behind a giant broom.

Soon the giant and his wife came in. The giant looked around the kitchen and cried,

Fe-fi-fo-fum,
I smell the blood of an . . .

His wife quickly ran to look in the oven, but no one was there.

The giant sat down in his chair with a thump that rattled the kitchen floor and called for his wife to bring him his magic harp. Jack watched as a lovely golden harp was set before the giant.

When the giant roared, "Sing!" the harp came to life and played a beautiful song all by itself. It even sang along with its music in a soft, sweet voice. The giant ate his supper while the harp played and sang. When the giant was full, the harp's music lulled him to sleep.

When the giant was snoring loudly and was certainly asleep, Jack crept from his hiding place behind the broom. He picked up the golden harp and ran away with it.

The magic harp called out, "Help, master!"

This woke the sleeping giant. When he realized that his prized harp was being stolen, the giant leaped up with a mighty roar of rage and grabbed for Jack with one of his huge hands.

Jack jumped off the table and ran just as fast as his legs would carry him. He could hear the tramp, tramp, tramp of the giant's boots behind him, and that made him run faster than he had ever run before!

When Jack reached the beanstalk, he climbed all the way down to the ground with the magic harp clutched tightly in one arm.

As soon as Jack reached the ground, he grabbed an ax and with one sharp blow chopped down the huge beanstalk. Down it crashed, and with it crashed the giant.

That was the end of the magic beanstalk and the end of the giant!

As for Jack and his mother, they lived happily ever after with the wonderful hen and the magical golden harp.

The
LITTLE
RED HEN

Adapted by Carolyn Quattrocki
Illustrated by Tim Ellis

Once upon a time, in a small, cozy little house, a little red hen lived with her chicks. The little red hen worked very hard taking care of her house and her family. She was a happy little hen, and she sang cheerful songs as she did her chores.

The little red hen had three friends—a cat, a dog, and a pig—who lived very near her. Every day she watched her three friends playing, but the little red hen didn't have time to play. She was too busy with her chicks and her house.

The little red hen started each day early in the morning. First she cooked breakfast for all her chicks. Then she made the beds and tended her garden. She cooked the meals, washed the clothes, and scrubbed the floors. She worked hard from morning till night.

But her three lazy friends—the cat, the dog, and the pig—never seemed to work at all. They went for long walks in the sunshine, lay about in the soft grass, and spent their time reading stories and playing games.

One sunny day the little red hen was outside working hard in her garden. She looked down at the ground where she was pulling some weeds, and she noticed some grains of wheat.

"Who will plant this wheat?" the little red hen asked her three friends.

"Not I," said the cat.

"Not I," said the dog.

"Not I," said the pig.

"Then I will do it myself," said the little red hen.

The little red hen planted the grains of wheat. Soon the wheat grew. The little red hen looked at the growing wheat and asked, "Who will help me tend this wheat?"

"Not I," said the cat.

"Not I," said the dog.

"Not I," said the pig.

"Then I will do it myself," said the little red hen to her three friends.

The days went by, and the little red hen worked very hard farming the wheat. She watered the field and hoed the ground and pulled the weeds. Finally the wheat was ripe and ready to be harvested.

The little red hen asked, "Who will help me cut all of this wheat?"

"Not I," said the cat.

"Not I," said the dog.

"Not I," said the pig.

"Then I will do it myself," said the little red hen.

The little red hen worked from morning to night cutting the golden wheat. When she finished harvesting all of the wheat, she loaded it onto her wagon.

The little red hen looked at the wagon filled with wheat and asked, "Who will help me take the wheat to the mill to be ground into flour?"

"Not I," said the cat.

"Not I," said the dog.

"Not I," said the pig.

"Then I will do it myself," said the little red hen to her three friends.

The little red hen walked a long way into the village.
She pulled her wagon of wheat behind her.

When she got to the village, she went to see the
miller. "Will you grind this wheat into flour for me?"
asked the little red hen.

"Oh yes," said the miller. "This wheat will make enough good flour for bread for all your chicks."

The miller ground the wheat into flour, and the little red hen set out for home. This time, in her wagon, she had a large sack of flour to make bread.

When the little red hen came back to her house, her three lazy friends were waiting for her. She showed them the flour.

"Now I shall bake some bread with the flour," said the little red hen. "Who will help me bake the bread?"

"Not I," said the cat.

"Not I," said the dog.

"Not I," said the pig.

"Then I will do it myself," said the little red hen, and

she began to wonder if the three were really friends.

When the bread was baked, the little red hen asked,

"Who will help me eat the bread?"

"I will!" said the cat.

"I will!" said the dog.

"I will!" said the pig.

But the little red hen stamped her foot and said angrily to the cat, the dog, and the pig, "Oh no. I found the wheat. I planted the wheat. I tended the wheat. I harvested the wheat. I took the wheat to be ground into flour. And I made the bread."

Then the little red hen said, "All these things I did by myself. Now my chicks and I will eat this bread all by ourselves!" And they did.

SNOW WHITE

Adapted by Jane Jerrard
Illustrated by Burgandy Nilles

Long ago in a far-off land, a princess was born with hair as black as night, skin as white as snow, and lips the color of rubies. She was called Snow White.

As the baby grew into a little girl, she became more beautiful every year. Her stepmother, the queen, was also very beautiful. The queen was so vain she had a magical mirror made. Every day she looked in the mirror and asked,

Mirror, mirror on the wall,
Who is fairest of us all?

The mirror would answer,

You, my queen, are fairest in the land.

And the queen was very pleased, because she knew that it was true.

But one day, when Snow White had grown to be a young maiden, the vain queen asked,

> *Mirror, mirror on the wall,*
> *Who is fairest of us all?*

And the mirror replied,

> *You, my queen, may lovely be,*
> *But Snow White is fairer still than thee.*

The queen was very angry, because she could not stand to have anyone be prettier than she. From that time on, the queen hated Snow White. When she could no longer bear to look at the beautiful princess, she called a woodsman and ordered him to take Snow White away and kill her.

The man, fearing for his own life, took the girl deep into the forest but could not bring himself to kill her. Instead he left Snow White there alone.

Snow White found herself all alone in the dark woods. Around her were mysterious noises and frightening shadows. She was so scared she began to run. Tree branches caught at her black hair as she ran through the forest. Wild beasts watched her, but they did not harm the beautiful girl.

She ran as fast and as far as she could, until she saw a little cottage with a red roof. When no one answered her knocks, Snow White went inside.

There she found a little table set with seven plates, and seven little beds were all lined up against the wall. The hungry princess nibbled a bit of food from each plate then threw herself down on the seventh bed and fell asleep.

Seven dwarfs shared this little cottage. Soon they came back from the gold and copper mines where they worked. How surprised they were to find Snow White sleeping in their home!

They let the lovely girl sleep until morning then asked her how she had found her way to their cottage deep in the woods. When they heard Snow White's story, they felt sorry for her and asked her to stay. She took care of the cottage, and the dwarfs gave her food, friendship, and shelter in return.

Snow White was happy living with the dwarfs. But one day back at the castle, the evil queen again asked,

Mirror, mirror on the wall,
Who is fairest of us all?

The mirror replied,

You, my queen, may lovely be,
But Snow White is fairer still than thee.

Then the queen knew that Snow White was still alive. She decided to kill the girl herself. The queen disguised herself as an ugly old woman and then appeared at the dwarfs' cottage. She called out, "Belts for sale! Buy my pretty belts!"

Snow White saw no danger in opening the door to let in the disguised queen. Snow White tried on one of the lovely silk belts. The queen pulled the belt so tight around the girl's waist that she fell down as if dead.

When the dwarfs returned, they found Snow White lying on the floor. Right away they saw that the girl's belt was too tight and cut it off with a knife. She began to breathe again and told them what had happened.

The dwarfs realized that the old woman must have been the evil queen, and they warned Snow White to be very careful. Above all she must not open the door to let in anyone.

Meanwhile, at the castle, the queen asked once more,

Mirror, mirror on the wall,
Who is fairest of us all?

When the mirror answered that Snow White was still the fairest, the queen shook with rage and vowed that Snow White must die.

The evil queen set out for the cottage in a new disguise. This time she offered to sell Snow White a lovely comb. Snow White took the comb—through the window this time—and put it in her hair. She fell right where she stood, because the comb was poisoned.

The dwarfs soon came home. They realized at once that the comb was poisoned and quickly removed it from Snow White's hair before it killed her. Back at the castle the queen asked yet again,

Mirror, mirror on the wall,
Who is fairest of us all?

When she learned that the princess still lived, the queen used all her magic to make a single perfect, poisoned apple.

Then the queen dressed herself as a poor woman and went once more to see Snow White. She offered the girl the apple, and Snow White could not resist it. Part of the apple's magic was that everyone who saw it must taste it. Snow White bit into the fruit, and she instantly fell down as if dead.

When the queen returned to the castle, her mirror told her at last, "Queen, thou art fairest of us all!"

The dwarfs could not wake Snow White, but she looked as healthy and as pretty as if she were comfortably sleeping. They laid her in a glass case so they could watch over her.

One day a prince was hunting in the woods. He came upon Snow White lying in the glass case and thought she was the most beautiful princess he had ever seen. He fell in love with her right away. He believed the glass box must be part of some evil enchantment, so he opened the case and lifted Snow White in his arms.

As the prince picked up Snow White, the piece of poisoned apple fell from her mouth, and she woke from her sleep. Snow White slowly opened her eyes to find herself in the arms of the prince!

When the dwarfs learned that Snow White was alive, they danced with joy and agreed happily that she should marry the prince.

As for the queen, her hatred made her so ugly that she could no longer bear to look in her mirror. She finally smashed it in a fit of rage, so she never found out about Snow White's happiness.

The THREE LITTLE PIGS

Adapted by Jane Jerrard

Illustrated by Susan Spellman

There once was a mother pig who told her three little pigs that it was now time for them to seek their fortunes. She warned them that each one must build a house to keep himself safe.

The first little pig met a man with a bundle of straw. He asked the man for some straw and built himself a little straw house. Soon enough a wolf came along and knocked on the door, saying, "Little pig, little pig, let me come in."

"Not by the hair of my chinny chin chin," answered the first little pig.

"Then I'll huff and I'll puff and I'll blow your house in!" said the wolf. And he huffed and he puffed and he blew the straw house down.

The first little pig was not safe in that house!

The second little pig met a man with a load of sticks. The pig decided to make his house out of sticks.

Along came the wolf, who knocked on his door and said, "Little pig, little pig, let me come in."

"Not by the hair of my chinny chin chin," answered the second little pig.

"Then I'll huff and I'll puff and I'll blow your house in!" And the wolf huffed and he puffed, and he huffed and he puffed again, and he blew the stick house down!

The second little pig was not safe in his house either!

The third little pig met a man with a load of bricks. He asked for some bricks and built a sturdy little house. Soon the big, bad wolf came knocking at his door, saying, "Little pig, little pig, let me come in."

"Not by the hair of my chinny chin chin," said the third little pig.

"Then I'll huff and I'll puff and I'll blow your house in!" said the wolf. So he huffed and he puffed, and he puffed and he huffed, and he huffed and he puffed! But he could not blow down the brick house.

When he saw that the house was still standing, the wolf gave up all his huffing and puffing. He sat down for a while and wondered how he could get his paws on that plump little pig, because he dearly wanted a plump pig for his dinner. Then he had an idea.

"Dear pig," he called, "come with me to Farmer Smith's turnip field. I happen to know that it is full of nice turnips. I will come for you at six o'clock tomorrow."

"All right," agreed the little pig. But the clever pig got up at five o'clock, went to Farmer Smith's, and gathered all the turnips he could carry. He was back home by six when the wolf arrived.

The wolf was very angry when he discovered that he had been tricked, but he did not show it. Instead he said politely, "Friend pig, I know of a lovely apple tree just up the hill. Its branches are heavy with ripe, delicious apples. I will come for you at five o'clock tomorrow. You must wait for me."

Of course, the little pig had a better idea. He awoke at four o'clock and hurried off to pick his apples, hoping to return before the wolf came. But this time he had to climb a tree, and it was not so easy to climb back down!

When the wolf arrived at the little pig's house, he was very angry to discover that he had been tricked once again! He decided to go to the apple tree anyway. The wolf was delighted to find that the little pig was still there, struggling to get down.

"Good morning, pig," said the wolf, licking his chops. "I am pleased to find you here. Tell me, are the apples as delicious as I said?"

"Let me throw you one," answered the pig, and he threw it as far down the hill as he could. When the wolf ran to get it, the pig managed to climb down and trotted home as fast as his little legs would carry him. There he baked himself a plump apple pie and had quite a feast.

The next day the wolf was back. He had thought of another way to get the pig to leave his house.

"Charming pig," he called, "won't you come with me to the fair this afternoon?"

"Oh, I love fairs!" said the pig. "What time will you stop by?"

"Three o'clock sharp," said the wolf.

The little pig slipped out early and went to the fair by himself. He had a wonderful time there. He admired the flowers, ate some cotton candy, and bought a nice barrel for his rainwater.

On the way home, with his new barrel, the pig saw the wolf coming along the road to meet him.

The pig climbed inside the barrel to hide, and it began to roll. It rolled right down the hill. The sight of the rolling barrel frightened the wolf so much that he turned and ran straight home!

The wolf came to the little pig's house later that day and told him how frightened he had been by the strange thing he had seen. The little pig laughed and said it had only been a barrel, and the pig himself had been inside it!

The big, bad wolf did not like being laughed at, and he was getting very hungry. No little pig was going to cheat him out of his dinner!

"Pig," he said, "I am tired of your tricks. The time has come to eat you up."

Because he could not huff and puff and blow that sturdy house down, the wicked wolf climbed onto the roof of the little pig's brick house. He shouted down the chimney, "Little pig, little pig, I'm coming in!"

When he heard this, the little pig hung a big pot of water over the fire.

The big, bad wolf came down the chimney and fell right into the boiling water. That was the end of the big, bad wolf!

The
TORTOISE
and the HARE

Adapted by Carolyn Quattrocki
Illustrated by Tim Ellis

Once upon a time, in a great forest, there lived a hare and a tortoise. Tortoise was slow with everything he did. He sometimes ate his breakfast so slowly that it was almost time for lunch before he had finished. He kept his house clean and neat, but he did it at his own pace, very slowly.

Hare, on the other hand, was quick as a wink in all that he did. He would be up in the morning, finished with his breakfast, and going for an early walk in the forest before Tortoise had gotten out of bed. Hare could not imagine how Tortoise could stand to be so slow all the time.

Tortoise lived next door to his good friend, Squirrel.

Squirrel had a cozy little home high up in an old oak tree.

She loved to spend her time scurrying around. She thought

it was fun to jump from branch to branch. Squirrel, like

Hare, wondered how Tortoise could always be so slow.

Hare lived near his old friend, Owl, who was not nearly as quick as Hare. In fact he spent a lot of his time sleeping. But Owl was a very wise and good neighbor. Sometimes he thought to himself, "Hare always seems to be rushing somewhere in a hurry. I wonder if he ever slows down?"

Every afternoon, when the weather was nice, Tortoise would gather up his paints and brushes, and go out into the woods. Tortoise loved to paint pictures of the flowers and trees and the stream near his house. He worked slowly, but his pictures were beautiful.

Hare thought painting a picture was not at all exciting.

"What a dull fellow Tortoise is!" he said. Hare had the most

fun leaping about the forest. He liked to visit his friends,

rushing from house to house. Wherever he went, he always

ran very, very fast.

There was just one problem. Hare was sure that he was the smartest, fastest, most handsome animal in the whole forest. And he never failed to tell his friends how splendid he was. "I think I look especially fine today," he would say to himself as he stood in front of his mirror.

Tortoise never bragged about himself. He knew that
he was not particularly handsome and that he was very
slow, but he did not mind. He was happy to spend his time
working hard, painting his beautiful pictures at his very
slow pace.

One day Tortoise was sitting beside the stream painting a picture of the pretty wildflowers on its bank. Hare came up and said, "You are such a slowpoke, Tortoise. You've been working on the same picture all week!"

"I'm not so very slow," protested Tortoise.

"Silly fellow," said Hare. "You're so slow that I could beat you at anything you can name. Just name something, and I'll win."

"All right," said Tortoise. "How about a race?"

What an idea! Hare laughed and laughed at the thought of running a race with Tortoise! Hare laughed so hard he thought he would explode.

Word of the race spread quickly through the forest. All the animals were talking about how Tortoise had boldly challenged Hare. "What was Tortoise thinking? Why did he do such a thing?" they wondered. Even Squirrel had to laugh at the idea of Tortoise racing Hare.

Squirrel hurried down her tree and went over to tell Owl the exciting news. When Owl heard about the big race, he blinked his eyes slowly and said in his deep, wise voice, "I am not so sure that Hare will win. You never can tell what is going to happen."

On the day of the big race, all the animals in the forest gathered at the starting line. Skunk and Chipmunk had been busy laying out the course for the race. Bear had a banner to mark the finish line. Squirrel had a bunch of balloons she was giving to the animals in the crowd.

Fox was to be the judge. "If the race is close, I will say who is the winner," he declared.

"Don't worry," said Hare. "You won't have a problem. I will be so far ahead, there will be no doubt about who is the winner of this race!"

Tortoise and Hare stepped up to the starting line.
Tortoise looked nervous when he saw all the animals.
Hare smiled and waved to the crowd. He could hardly
wait to show Tortoise a thing or two about running a race.

Fox looked at both runners. He shouted, "Get ready.
Get set. GO!"

The race was on! Hare dashed across the starting line. In the blink of an eye, he disappeared over the first hill.

"Oh dear," said Squirrel to herself. "There goes Hare, out of sight already. Poor Tortoise hasn't even started!" Sure enough, Tortoise was just beginning to climb the steep path—very slowly.

Hare ran and ran until he was sure he would win.
"This isn't even a race," he said to himself. "I think I'll lie
down and rest a bit. Then I'll finish and still have plenty
of time to spare. There's no way that slowpoke will ever
catch up with me!" So Hare lay down under a shady tree
and soon fell fast asleep.

Suddenly Hare awoke with a start. He could hear cheering. He leaped to his feet and began running as fast as his long legs would carry him. But when he saw the finish line of the race, he could not believe his eyes.

Tortoise was about to win the race. Hare could not believe it. Tortoise was crossing the finish line!

The crowd cheered and cheered. They ran to the finish line to congratulate Tortoise. The wise Owl blinked his eyes and said what all the other animals were thinking, "Slow and steady wins the race!"

The
STEADFAST
TIN SOLDIER

Adapted by Bette Killion
Illustrated by Jim Salvati

Once upon a time, there were twenty-five tin soldiers in a wooden box. Each was brave. Each was handsome and wore a smart, blue uniform. One soldier, Will, had only a single leg. He had been made last, and the toy maker had run out of tin.

Will stood just as straight on his one leg as the others did on two, and he was just as brave and handsome.

The tin soldiers were given to a boy on his birthday. Will looked around and found that he was in a nursery. There were many other toys in the room. On the far side of the table, he saw a castle made of paper. In the doorway of the castle stood a beautiful paper maiden. Will fell in love with her at once.

The paper maiden, whose name was Alyssa, was a very graceful dancer. One arm was raised above her head, and one foot was lifted so high behind her that Will thought she had only one leg, just like him. She wore a dress made of sky blue gauze with a blue ribbon on one sleeve.

"She would make a perfect wife for me," thought Will. He gazed and gazed at the paper maiden, unable to take his eyes off her.

Evening came, and the boy put all the soldiers except Will back in the box. When it grew dark, the toys began to play together. The tin soldier stood stiffly at attention and watched Alyssa. She stood still and looked at him out of the corner of her eye.

The next morning the boy took the soldier and stood him on the windowsill. All of a sudden, a gust of wind blew. Will fell out of the window, and his hat stuck in the dirt between stones in the street below.

Soon it began to rain. The rain came down so hard that water ran in torrents down the street. Will bravely waited for the downpour to end. When it was over, two boys found the toy soldier. They made a paper boat, put Will in it, and floated him down a canal.

The canal emptied into a dark tunnel. The waters were so swift that the paper boat whirled and tipped dangerously, but the tin soldier held fast and was very brave. How he wished that the beautiful Alyssa could be here with him! Then he would have been happy.

A big rat who lived in the tunnel suddenly loomed up beside the boat.

"Where is your pass?" the rat demanded. "Give me your pass at once."

The tin soldier remained still and steady. The rat swam as fast as he could, but the boat whirled away too fast in the current.

Soon the rat was left behind. Will could hear the sound of the rat's voice fading as the boat whirled on. He let out a great sigh of relief.

Will wondered what was in store for him next and if he would ever see the beautiful Alyssa again. The current grew stronger and stronger, pulling the boat along faster and faster. Just as Will began to see daylight at the end of the tunnel, he heard a terrible splashing. Will's boat was heading straight for a waterfall.

He knew the poor, soggy boat could never survive a waterfall, but there was no avoiding it. He pulled himself up and stood more bravely than ever on his one leg.

Once the soggy paper boat was caught in the rushing waterfall, it quickly filled with water and sank.

"This must certainly be my end," thought the tin soldier as he plunged swiftly down into the whirlpool. "I will never again see the beautiful Alyssa, nor will I ever know how wonderful it would have been to watch her dance for me."

Round and round he whirled. His shiny blue uniform caught the eye of a large fish. The fish stopped, looked Will over from head to toe, and then swallowed him in one gulp.

It was much darker in the fish than in the tunnel, but Will held himself as straight as he could. The fish seemed to dash around frantically for a time and then lay quiet.

After a long time there was a flash like lightning, and Will saw daylight again. The fish had been caught on someone's hook. Now it was in a kitchen, and the cook was preparing it for dinner.

"My goodness! Look at this tin soldier inside my fish!" exclaimed the cook. She pulled Will out, then wiped him off and brought him to the nursery.

Will looked around and saw the box where his brothers were and the paper castle. His heart started to beat faster when he realized that he was home. The boy came into the nursery and looked at the tin soldier.

"Where have you been?" the little boy asked him in an accusing tone. "You're damp, and you smell like a fish."

Suddenly he opened the window and tossed Will into the flower garden below. Will lay among the petunias and felt sad, but he remained brave.

Just then a gentle wind blew over him. It blew through the house, caught up Alyssa, and blew her straight out the open window into the garden.

With a graceful little flutter, the paper dancer landed next to Will among the petunias.

The two looked at each other with beating hearts and adoring eyes. Then they slid very close together.

"Will you stay with me and be my wife?" Will asked.

"Yes, forever and ever!" she whispered.

And that is exactly what Alyssa did. Will and Alyssa
were married beneath the leaves of a low-growing plant.

Sometimes, when the moon shone through the branches
above and the air was balmy and warm, the graceful Alyssa
would dance for her husband.

She always remained true to Will, as did the Steadfast
Tin Soldier to her.

CINDERELLA

Adapted by Jane Jerrard
Illustrated by Susan Spellman

Once upon a time, there was a young girl, as sweet as sugared milk, as kind as a mother's kiss, and as pretty as a sun setting in the sky.

The girl had a very mean stepmother who made her life a misery. The stepmother and her two nasty daughters treated the girl as a servant. They always made her scrub the floors and wash the dishes and pick up after them. They called the girl Cinderella because at day's end she would sit among the cinders on the hearth and warm her tired bones.

Cinderella was always cheerful and polite, even though her stepsisters treated her cruelly. Her kindness made her beautiful, and her beauty shone like sunlight through the dirt on her face and her ragged clothing.

One day something very exciting arrived. It was an invitation to the prince's fancy ball! All the fine people in the land were invited, and the sisters worried about what to wear and how to behave with royalty.

Poor Cinderella sewed and ironed for days, but she herself was not going to the ball. She was only a servant. Besides she did not have a gown nice enough for a ball.

Finally the great night arrived. As Cinderella helped her younger stepsister into her gown, the cruel girl asked, "Cinderella, why don't you come with us to the ball and dance with the prince?"

The stepmother and her daughters laughed at the thought of dirty, barefoot Cinderella dancing with the handsome prince.

As the stepmother and her daughters rode off to the ball, Cinderella cried a few tears. Suddenly a beautiful fairy magically appeared from thin air. It was Cinderella's fairy godmother!

"What is wrong, dear Cinderella?" asked her fairy godmother. Even though she had secretly watched over Cinderella's hard life, this was the first time she had ever seen the girl cry.

Cinderella explained that she wanted very much to go to the ball to meet the prince.

"And so you shall go, Cinderella, for you have always, always been good!" said her fairy godmother.

With her special magic, Cinderella's fairy godmother turned a hollow pumpkin into a beautiful coach. Then she found six mice, and waving her wand over them, she turned them into six fine, gray horses, ready to pull Cinderella's carriage. All that was missing was a driver. A fat, white rat was just the thing!

"Now, sweet girl, you can go to the ball!" said the fairy godmother.

"But my clothes . . . ," whispered Cinderella. "I cannot go to the ball in dirty rags!"

With one touch of her sparkling wand, her fairy godmother turned Cinderella's old dress into a lovely gown trimmed in gold and silver. Best of all she gave the girl a pair of tiny glass slippers that fit just right!

With the help of the footman, Cinderella stepped into the waiting magical-pumpkin coach. A shiver of excitement ran through her. Was this a dream? She pinched herself and decided that it was not.

Just before the coach pulled away, Cinderella's fairy godmother spoke. "You must be home before midnight, Cinderella," she warned, "because my magic will disappear when the clock strikes twelve o'clock!"

Cinderella promised her fairy godmother that she would not be late, and off she rode to the ball. The whole way there, her heart was pounding with anticipation!

Cinderella stepped out of her coach and gracefully climbed the stairs to the palace. When she appeared in the doorway to the ballroom, the other guests hushed as she was escorted down the staircase.

The prince took one look at her and fell in love with beautiful Cinderella. In fact, everyone at the ball fell in love with her. As the prince and Cinderella danced, all the people smiled and watched. No one recognized her, not even her stepsisters and stepmother.

The prince asked Cinderella to dance every dance. Cinderella was so happy she forgot the time. The clock had nearly finished striking the hour of midnight when Cinderella remembered the promise she had made to her fairy godmother.

Cinderella dashed out of the ballroom, leaving the prince and the rest of the guests astonished! She ran down the palace steps in such a hurry that she left one of her glass slippers behind.

The prince ran after Cinderella, but it was too late. She had disappeared into the shadows. He wanted to call out to her, but he realized that she had never told him her name! The prince found a glass slipper on the palace steps and vowed to find its mysterious owner.

Cinderella ran all the way home, dressed in her rags. Her coach had turned back into a pumpkin, and the mice and the rat had all run away. All she had left was the other glass slipper.

The next day everyone in the land could talk of nothing but the ball and the beautiful stranger who had stolen the prince's heart.

The prince was very unhappy. He had fallen in love with someone wonderful, but he did not know her name or anything about her.

"This tiny glass slipper is all that I have," he thought. "I must use it to try to find her." That very day he began to search over all the land, trying to find the maiden who could wear the delicate glass slipper.

The prince and his servants went from house to house, inviting every woman—young or old—to try the slipper. But not one foot fit into it!

At last the young prince arrived at the house where Cinderella lived with her stepmother and two stepsisters. He was weary from his search and was beginning to think that he would never find the woman he loved.

The stepsisters both tried to fit their large feet into the slipper. It was plain to see that neither of these ladies was the mysterious stranger from the ball.

Cinderella had been watching from beside the fire. She asked softly, "May I please try?" Her stepmother and stepsisters laughed and told her not to waste the prince's precious time.

The prince knelt and held out the glass slipper for Cinderella. Her foot slipped into it with ease! Cinderella had carefully kept the other glass slipper. Now she pulled it from her apron pocket and put it on, too.

The stepmother and stepsisters were astonished.

"It fits!" shrieked the stepmother.

"It fits!" howled the stepsisters.

"It fits!" sang Cinderella's fairy godmother, who had been watching all along. She once again waved her wand and dressed Cinderella in a beautiful gown.

Cinderella went back to the palace with the prince. He was so overcome with love and joy that he married her that very day!

The
UGLY
DUCKLING

Adapted by Jane Jerrard

Illustrated by Susan Spellman

Once there was a little farm, with a pond full of geese and ducks. On a fine morning in May, a duck sitting on her nest full of eggs felt something start to move underneath her—crack, crack, crack.

Peep, peep! Her eggs were starting to hatch. She was very glad, because it seemed as though she had been sitting on the nest for a long, long time.

One by one her little ducklings broke through their eggshells, each fluffier and softer than the one before it. Finally the last egg started to crack open. It was a very big egg, and the duckling that came out was large and clumsy and a dirty gray color. He did not look at all like any of the other ducklings!

The mother duck thought, "How big and ugly this duckling is!" But she loved him just the same. When the mother duck led her babies to the pond, the ugly duckling swam just as well as the rest, so she didn't worry about him any longer.

The next day the mother duck took her babies to the farmyard for the first time. The proud duck lined up her ducklings in a neat row, with the ugly duckling at the very end, and told them to quack properly and bow their heads to everyone they met.

When the duck family entered the farmyard where the plump chickens, ducks, and geese were gathered, the other ducks were quite rude.

"Look at that ugly little fellow! He's not one of us!" said one snowy white duck. A mean old goose even reached out and bit the ugly duckling on the neck.

"Leave him alone!" cried the mother duck, but the other birds continued to tease the poor duckling. Soon even his own brothers and sisters were calling him "ugly duckling" and wouldn't play with him.

Days passed, and the duckling grew bigger and uglier. The teasing and bullying got worse and worse. Finally the duckling decided to run far away. He wandered through overgrown fields, often frightening the little birds who lived there.

"They think I'm ugly, too," he sighed.

On he went, until he came to a swamp where wild geese lived. Since he was too tired to go any farther, he stayed there for the night. The wild geese found him in the morning.

"What kind of bird are you?" they asked. Before he could answer, some men came with their dogs and scared the geese away. The ugly duckling hid in the grass, because he was too frightened to leave.

As soon as he was sure the dogs were gone, the lonely little duckling set off again, looking for somewhere to live. At last he came to a crooked little hut, where an old woman lived with her cat and her prized hen. She took the duckling in, hoping he would grow fat. She thought she could sell him at market.

The cat and the hen thought that they were wonderful creatures and were very rude to the duckling. Besides he was used to being outdoors, and although the hut was warm and dry, he longed to be swimming on the water and diving down among the weeds.

So one fall day he ran away to find a lake.

Find one the ugly duckling did. He was happy on the lake, although none of the wild ducks there spoke to him. They thought he was too ugly to bother with.

One day at sunset he saw a flock of beautiful birds flying overhead. Their feathers were so white they glowed, and their necks were long and graceful. The sight of them made the ugly duckling cry, although he did not know why.

Soon afterward the wild ducks flew off. They knew that winter was coming. The duckling stayed on the lake as the weather got colder and colder. It grew so cold one night that the duckling awoke to find his feet frozen in a sheet of ice!

Luckily a farmer found the duckling held fast there and broke the ice to free him. The kind farmer took the duckling home with him, thinking the odd bird would make a fine pet for his children.

When the farmer set the duckling down in his kitchen, the noisy children frightened the bird, and the duckling flew right into a pail of milk and spilled it. From there he ran across a plate of butter and knocked over a bowl of flour. What a mess he made!

The farmer's wife was angry with the ugly duckling and chased him right out the kitchen door.

The frightened duckling did not run very far, because it was dark and cold outside. He knew the icy pond was not a safe place to spend the winter, so he found a safe hiding place in an empty barnyard and made a nest for himself.

The ugly duckling spent the whole winter nestled snug in his hiding place. He came out only to search for food. It was the longest, loneliest winter he could imagine.

Spring came at last! The ugly duckling stretched his neck and tried to fly. His wings were now very strong, and he landed easily on his little lake!

Just as the ugly duckling was enjoying his first swim of the spring, three snowy swans appeared from the grass along the shore. The duckling felt the same excitement he had felt when he had first seen them flying overhead.

He wanted to be near them so much that, even though he was sure they would treat him cruelly, he swam toward them anyway. As he drew near, he bowed his head, ready for the name-calling and biting he had learned to expect from other birds.

When he lowered his head, what do you think he saw? A fourth swan, the most beautiful of all, was looking back at him from the water. It was his own reflection!

You see, over that long winter the ugly duckling had grown up. He was not a duckling at all. He was a swan!

As the other swans joined him, the happy bird promised himself that he would never forget the things he had learned as the ugly duckling, even though he would spend the rest of his life as a handsome swan.

The PIED PIPER of HAMELIN

Adapted by Carolyn Quattrocki

Illustrated by Tim Ellis

Once upon a time, far away and long ago, there was a town called Hamelin. It was a pleasant little town with a river on one side and a high mountain on the other.

The people of Hamelin liked living there because they always had plenty to eat and drink. Their children were healthy and happy.

One day the people of Hamelin saw that they had a very serious problem. Their lovely town was full of rats! Everywhere the people went, there were rats. Rats were in the trees, the streets, the alleys, the attics, and the cellars. There were even rats on the tops of houses. In short, rats were practically everywhere!

Rats went into the kitchens and bothered the cooks.

They nibbled the bread and cakes. They ate the cheeses,

drank the soup, and ruined the pies.

As soon as one rat was chased away, three more came

to take its place!

Rats fought with the dogs and bit the cats. They made
their nests everywhere in town, even in the gentlemen's hats.
They were so noisy that ladies having their tea together
could scarcely hear each others' voices.

What on earth were the poor people of Hamelin to do?

The most important man in the town was the mayor.

It was his job to see that everything ran smoothly.

The mayor was a wealthy man who loved to eat the

richest food and drink the finest wine. He wore a cape of

fur, a cap of fine feathers, and costly rings on his fingers.

He thought himself a splendid fellow.

To help him with his job of running the town, the mayor had a council. The mayor and his council met each week to talk about all the things that needed to be done in the town. The weekly meetings in the town hall were festive occasions. They always had a feast of good food and wine.

One day the townspeople said to themselves, "We have had enough of these rats in our town! The mayor and his council sit and do nothing, while the rats are everywhere. Something must be done!"

With that a large crowd of people gathered before the town hall and cried out, "Let us see the mayor!"

In his office the mayor heard the people's complaints.
He knew how awful it was to have rats everywhere in town.
His own house was full of them.

Sadly the mayor did not have the slightest idea of how
to fix the problem. None of the members of his council
did either.

Suddenly there was a knock on the mayor's door. The people all turned to see a strange fellow standing there. He was wearing a long, red cape and a hat with a red feather. He had yellow hair, and a pipe hung from a silk scarf around his neck.

"I am a poor piper," he said, "but I can rid your town of rats. Would you pay a hundred pieces of gold for me to do it?"

"Oh, I would give a thousand pieces of gold to anyone who could rid us of these rats!" exclaimed the mayor.

And the rest of the council members echoed, "Yes, yes. A thousand pieces of gold!"

The pied piper stepped into the town square and began to play. How beautiful and sweet was his music! Suddenly rats came running to him from all directions. Big rats, small rats, thin rats, fat rats, old rats, and young rats came running. Before long he had a whole army of rats behind him.

Through the town and to the edge of the river, the
rats followed the pied piper. At the river's edge he paused,
but the rats kept running. Without stopping, every single
rat jumped into the river and drowned.

The people were astonished. All the rats were gone!
They cheered as the piper walked back to the town hall.

To the astonished mayor the pied piper said, "I have come to collect my thousand pieces of gold."

"But sir," cried the mayor, "that was only a joke! Surely you could not expect us to pay a thousand pieces of gold for such short work! Here are twenty-five pieces."

"You promised one thousand," said the pied piper.

"All right, here are fifty pieces. Take them and be gone," said the mayor.

At that the pied piper began to play his pipe again. He went down to the town square, and this time the children heard the music and came running to him from all directions.

Before the pied piper had blown more than a few notes on his pipe, the sound of many small running feet could be heard.

The children listened, and the beautiful music was so sweet to their ears that they could not help themselves. They ran to the place where the pied piper was playing.

From each street more children came. Small children, large children, brothers, sisters, and little babies carried by older children, they all ran to the pied piper. Little hands clapped to the music. Small feet danced to the merry tune. What a parade they made. A long line of dancing children had formed behind the pied piper.

Soon all the children in the town were following the pied piper. He led them toward the river. The people were suddenly afraid. Would their children jump in the river as the rats had done? The pied piper turned and headed toward the mountain. The people thought he would never be able to lead their children over such a high mountain.

Just then the pied piper and the long line of dancing children reached the mountain. The townspeople were amazed as a magical door suddenly opened in the side of the rock.

As the townspeople watched, the pied piper led all the children of Hamelin through the door in the mountain.

The poor people of Hamelin cried as they watched the
pied piper lead their children through the door, never to be
seen again. They were sad for what their mayor had done.
The children of Hamelin went to live beyond the mountain
in a land that was always filled with happiness and laughter
and sunshine.

The
SLEEPING
BEAUTY

Adapted by Jane Jerrard

Illustrated by Burgandy Nilles

Once upon a time in a far-off land, there lived a good king and queen who wanted a child more than anything in the world. After many wishful years the queen at last gave birth to a little daughter, and the whole land joined in the parents' happiness.

The king invited all the people in the kingdom to a great party, and the queen asked seven fairies to be the baby girl's godmothers.

The fairies were all invited to the party. Each fairy was to give the new princess a magical gift.

The seven fairies sat at a fine table. Each place at the table was set with golden plates and cups decorated with diamonds and rubies.

But there was another fairy—a very old fairy—whom the queen had forgotten to invite. As the guests sat down, this fairy appeared among them. She was very angry at having been forgotten, so the queen apologized and quickly ordered another place set for her. But there were no more golden plates or jeweled cups. The old fairy had to eat off fine china and sip from a crystal glass. This made her even angrier than before.

The beautiful young fairy who sat beside her at the fine table heard the evil old woman muttering to herself during dinner, and she decided to hide behind the curtains in case the old fairy caused some mischief.

Before long the time came for the godmothers to give their gifts. "I give this child beauty," said the first fairy.

"She shall be as good as she is lovely," said the second fairy godmother.

"She shall have happiness all her days," offered the third. The princess was also given gifts of a quick mind, dancing feet, and a beautiful voice.

Then the old fairy stepped forward. She was angry at having been forgotten by the queen. "I give this princess a curse. On her sixteenth birthday she will prick her finger on the spindle of a spinning wheel and die."

The guests, the king and queen, and the seven fairies shook with fear at the terrible curse. Then the seventh fairy stepped out from her hiding place.

"I cannot take away this curse," she said, "but I can change it. The princess will not die when the spindle pricks her finger. Instead she will fall into a deep sleep that will last at least a hundred years. Our princess will awaken only by the kiss of a king's son."

The king and queen found little comfort in the seventh fairy's gift. The king ordered all the spinning wheels in his kingdom destroyed to try to save his little daughter from the frightful curse.

Many years later, on the day of her sixteenth birthday, the princess was exploring the castle. At the top of the tallest tower, she came upon a little room where an old woman sat spinning thread. The princess, who had never seen anyone spin before, asked the old woman what she was doing.

"I am spinning, my dear," replied the woman.

"How clever!" said the girl. "Please let me try."

The princess sat down at the spinning wheel to try it for herself. But as soon as she started to spin, she pricked her finger on the spindle and at once fell into a deep sleep.

No one in the kingdom could wake the sleeping beauty. So they dressed her in a fine white gown and laid her in her royal bed.

When the seventh fairy heard that the curse had come to pass, she flew to the kingdom. She knew that the princess would be frightened to wake up among strangers, so she touched everybody in the kingdom with her magic wand. The fairy touched all the servants and the king and queen. She even touched the princess' little dog. Everyone she touched fell fast asleep and would not awaken until the princess' eyes opened.

Last of all she grew a magical forest of thorny trees around the castle to protect it. Then everything was still for a hundred years.

As the years passed people forgot the castle hidden in the woods. Then one day a young prince was out riding over the hills. He noticed a tower rising above the trees.

"What is that castle I see in the woods?" he asked the people he met.

But no one knew. Finally a very old man told the prince a tale that his father had told him about the hidden castle. It was the story of the sleeping beauty.

The prince grew very excited upon hearing this tale and decided to rescue the beautiful princess. He was ready to cut his way through the thorny forest to reach her, but the trees parted magically to make a path for him—a path right to the castle door!

The prince bravely entered the castle. Everywhere he looked, he saw people sleeping soundly. Cooks snored loudly in the kitchen, maids slept upon their brooms, and the king dreamed on his throne.

The prince searched through the entire enchanted castle before he found the princess, lying in her bed of gold and silver. At the sight of her, he leaned down and kissed her cheek.

The princess opened her eyes. When she saw the handsome young man, she smiled and asked, "Is it you, my prince?"

The prince was charmed at the sound of her voice and told her that, indeed, he had come to save her. Then he told her that he loved her already for he had dreamed of this meeting.

The two spoke for a very long time, but they were so excited and happy that their words made little sense.

The prince and princess were interrupted by a great cheer. The whole castle was awake! The king and queen came to find their daughter, and they thanked the young prince for breaking the enchantment. The king called for a great celebration.

The entire kingdom celebrated their awakening with a party that lasted for many days and many nights, since they were not sleepy at all!

At the end of the party, the princess and prince were married in the palace, and their life together was happier than they had dreamed possible.

RUMPELSTILTSKIN

Adapted by Jane Jerrard

Illustrated by Burgandy Nilles

Long ago, in a time of kings and castles, there lived a poor miller and his beautiful daughter.

The miller was a foolish old man who could not stop himself from bragging. His friends told him that his talk would get him into trouble, and they were right.

One day the miller was lucky enough to meet the king. He bragged to the great man that his lovely daughter could spin straw into gold.

The king, though rich, always wanted more gold, so he asked the miller's daughter to come to his castle that very day.

When the miller's daughter arrived, the king led her to a little room filled with straw. He gave her a spinning wheel and told her that if she could spin all the straw into gold by morning, he would make her his queen. But if she could not, her father must be killed for lying to the king.

He then left her all alone, locked in the little room filled with straw. As soon as the king left, the miller's daughter sat down and started to cry. She had no idea how to spin straw into gold.

Suddenly the door flew open, and there stood a funny little man.

"Good evening, pretty child," he said with a little bow. "What makes you so sad?"

She told him about her impossible task and the terrible fate that awaited her father if she could not spin the straw into gold.

"Well, I can spin straw into gold," said the little man, as if it were the easiest thing in the world. "But what will you give me for my work?"

"You may have my necklace," she said.

So the little man started working at the spinning wheel. He spun and spun, and soon the miller's daughter fell asleep. When she woke up, she was greeted by an amazing sight. During the night the little man had spun every bit of straw into gold.

The king was amazed to see the spools of gold awaiting him the following morning, but he did not make the miller's daughter his queen. Instead he took her to a much larger room filled with straw and ordered her to spin it into gold. If she could not, he warned her, her father must be killed.

The poor miller's daughter was once again left all alone, and she began to cry. She still did not know how to spin gold from straw. Suddenly the door opened, and there again stood the strange little man!

"More straw?" he asked. "What can you give me to spin it into gold?"

"The ring from my finger," she answered. So the little man worked through the long night and spun every piece of straw into gold.

The next day the king could not believe his eyes when he saw the room full of gold. He led the miller's daughter to a third room—one of the largest in his castle—filled to the ceiling with straw. There he left her, and she waited for the little man to appear.

The strange little man came soon enough, but this time she had nothing left to give him.

"Give me your first child when you become queen," said the little man.

The miller's daughter agreed, because she did not believe she would ever marry the king.

But the next morning, when the king saw the huge room filled with gold, he did marry her, and she became the queen.

A year later the king and queen had a beautiful baby. The queen had forgotten all about the promise she made to the little man. But the very first day she held her new baby, he appeared once more before her.

"I have come for the child," said the little man.

The queen wept and begged and offered him all the riches of her kingdom if she could just keep her new baby. Feeling sorry for her, the little man told her that she could have three days and nights to guess his name. If she guessed right, she could keep her baby.

All that night the queen sat up and made a list of every name she knew. Then she sent her servants out to discover new names she had not heard before. The servants roamed the country asking people their names and making lists for the queen.

When the strange little man returned the next evening, the queen called out names one at a time. "Are you Tom? Dick? Harry?" The little man shook his head no.

"Are you Gaspar? Melchior? Balthasar?" At each name, the little man just smiled and shook his head.

On the second day the servants came back with all the strangest names they had heard in the kingdom that day. When the little man appeared that night, the queen asked him, "Are you Cowribs? Spindleshanks? Lacelegs?"

But he only grinned and shook his head.

The third day, one servant returned without a list of names, but he told the queen a strange story. He had seen an odd little man dancing around a campfire, singing,

Today I brew, and then I bake,
And soon the queen's own child I'll take.
For little knows my royal dame
That RUMPELSTILTSKIN is my name!

That night the little man came to the palace with a big smile on his face. He was quite certain that the queen could never guess his name. He asked gleefully if she had any guesses left unguessed.

"Are you Klaus?" she asked.

"No," was his impish reply.

"Could you be Heinz?"

"No," giggled the little man.

"Perhaps you are RUMPELSTILTSKIN?" asked the queen with a wide smile.

The little man could not believe his ears. How could the queen have guessed his name? He grew so angry that he stamped his feet until he stamped through the floor!

And that was the last ever seen of Rumpelstiltskin.

The THREE BILLY GOATS GRUFF

Adapted by Carolyn Quattrocki

Illustrated by Tim Ellis

Once there were three Billy Goats Gruff. The oldest was Big Billy Goat Gruff who wore a collar of thick black braid. Middle Billy Goat Gruff had a red collar around his neck, and Little Billy Goat Gruff wore a yellow one.

Big Billy Goat Gruff had a deep, gruff billy goat voice.

Middle Billy Goat Gruff had a middle-size billy goat voice. And Little Billy Goat Gruff had a very high, little billy goat voice.

All winter long, the three Billy Goats Gruff lived on a rocky hillside. Right next to their hill ran a powerful, rushing river.

Every day during the cold winter months, the three
Billy Goats Gruff played among the rocks.

Little Billy Goat Gruff would cry in his little billy goat
voice, "Watch this!" as he leaped over little rocks.

Middle Billy Goat Gruff would call,

"Watch this!" as he leaped over middle-size rocks.

Big Billy Goat Gruff would say in his big billy goat

voice, "WATCH THIS!" as he leaped over great big rocks.

At night the wind would blow cold over the three Billy Goats Gruff. Little Billy Goat Gruff looked up to see a sky filled with bright, shining stars.

Middle Billy Goat Gruff looked up at the night to see the thin sliver of a winter moon.

Big Billy Goat Gruff said, "Enough looking at the sky, it is time to find a place to sleep."

So the three Billy Goats Gruff found a nice, cozy cave to sleep in. They lay down together on the cold winter nights and dreamed of springtime.

Soon it was springtime. From their rocky hillside the three Billy Goats Gruff looked longingly across the rushing river.

"How I would love to go up the mountain across the river," said Little Billy Goat Gruff. "The grass is green, and the flowers are pretty. There is plenty to eat on that side."

"To get to the mountain," said Middle Billy Goat Gruff, "we will have to cross the bridge over the river."

The three Billy Goats Gruff knew that under the bridge lived a great, ugly troll. The troll had eyes that were as big as saucers, a head of shaggy hair, and a nose that was as long as a broomstick.

Every day the Billy Goats Gruff looked across the river.

"The grass looks so sweet over there!" said Little Billy

Goat Gruff. "Let's go over the bridge."

"The flowers smell like honey!" said Middle Billy Goat

Gruff. "Yes, let's go over the bridge."

"But what are we to do about the troll?" asked Big
Billy Goat Gruff. They all shook their heads sadly.

One day, as they were looking at the green mountain,
Big Billy Goat Gruff had an idea. He thought of a plan to
trick the troll so that they could cross the bridge to the
other side.

~§

The next morning the three Billy Goats Gruff went down to the river. Little Billy Goat Gruff started to cross the bridge.

Trip-trap, trip-trap, trip-trap, went Little Billy Goat Gruff's feet on the bridge.

"Who's that trip-trapping across my bridge?" roared the troll.

"It is only I, Little Billy Goat Gruff," said Little Billy Goat Gruff.

"I'm coming to eat you up!" said the troll.

"Oh no!" said Little Billy Goat Gruff. "I am only a tiny, little billy goat. Wait for my brother, Middle Billy Goat Gruff. He will make a much bigger dinner for you."

So the troll let Little Billy Goat Gruff cross the bridge to the other side.

In a little while Middle Billy Goat Gruff started across the bridge. Trip-trap, trip-trap, trip-trap went Middle Billy Goat Gruff's feet as he walked across the bridge.

"Who's that trip-trapping across my bridge?" roared the troll.

"It is only I, Middle Billy Goat Gruff," he said.

"I'm coming to eat you up!" said the troll.

"Oh no!" said Middle Billy Goat Gruff. "I am only a middle-size billy goat. Wait for my brother, Big Billy Goat Gruff. He will make a much bigger dinner for you to eat."

The troll let Middle Billy
Goat Gruff cross the bridge
to the other side.

Finally Big Billy Goat
Gruff crossed the bridge.
TRIP-TRAP, TRIP-TRAP,
TRIP-TRAP went Big Billy
Goat Gruff as he walked on
the bridge.

"Who's TRIP-TRAPPING
across my bridge?" roared
the troll.

"It is I, Big Billy Goat Gruff," he said.

I'm coming to eat you up!" said the troll.

"Come ahead!" said Big Billy Goat Gruff. So the troll climbed up onto the bridge. Then Big Billy Goat Gruff, with his two big horns, tossed the troll high into the air, and he fell down into the river below.

The three Billy Goats Gruff were happy to be on the
other side. They feasted on the green grass and wildflowers.

"I was right," said Little Billy Goat Gruff. "The grass
tastes as sweet as it smells."

"And I was right, too," said Middle Billy Goat Gruff.
"The flowers are like honey."

"Best of all, I was right," said Big Billy Goat Gruff.

"We tricked the evil troll and used the bridge."

So the three Billy Goats Gruff spent their summer

happily eating in the high meadows. They grew very fat

and contented.

When the weather began to grow cold again in the autumn, the three fat Billy Goats Gruff came down from the high meadows.

This time they crossed over the bridge without a worry. After Big Billy Goat Gruff tossed him into the river, the wicked troll was never seen again.

BEAUTY
and the
BEAST

Adapted by Jane Jerrard
Illustrated by Burgandy Nilles

There once was a rich man who had six children—three daughters and three sons. After a lifetime of good luck, the man suddenly fell upon hard times. His house burned down, his ships sank at sea, and his business partner ran off with all his money.

He and his children were forced to move into a small cottage in the country, where they lived on food that they raised themselves. His two oldest daughters were unhappy with this change, but the youngest, named Beauty, tried to make their new life as comfortable as possible.

One day the man heard that one of his ships had sailed safely into harbor. He decided to go to the port to see this for himself, even though it was a long ride.

His children asked their father to bring back expensive presents for them, but Beauty asked only for her father's safe return.

"Isn't there anything I can bring you, Beauty?" asked her father.

"If you see one, I would like to have a rose," she said, for Beauty missed the beautiful gardens of their old home.

Beauty's father reached the port safely, only to find that his ship had been robbed and that he was now poorer than before. Making his way back home through a thick forest, the unlucky man was lost in a terrible snowstorm.

Suddenly, up ahead, he saw a row of flowering trees and at the same time felt warm air on his face!

The father had stumbled upon an enchanted castle. He explored the gardens, where no snow had fallen, then went inside, even though no one would answer the door.

He found a cheerful little room with a table of fresh food waiting for him. He ate hungrily then fell asleep in front of the fire.

The next morning there was still no sign of anyone, so the man got ready to leave. On his way through the gardens, he picked a rose for Beauty. Suddenly an awful beast appeared, as if by magic! "Is this how you thank me? I feed and shelter you and then you steal from me?" said the beast.

The man begged for his life, explaining that the rose was for one of his daughters.

The beast said that he would not kill the man but would accept one of his daughters instead. He promised to treat her kindly if she would come to live with him.

The man returned home and told his children what had happened. All six agreed that since Beauty's rose had started the trouble, she must be the one to go. The very next day, she rode away bravely with her father.

Again they found no one in the enchanted castle, and again supper was set on the table. But this time the beast appeared as they finished eating. Beauty was frightened by the beast's terrible face, but he spoke to her gently, asking if she would stay with him to save her father's life.

Beauty told the beast she would stay. So her father left her there, although it broke his heart, and she made the beast's castle her home. Beauty had her own big room with mirrors for walls and a clock that woke her by calling out her name. She spent her days alone, exploring the wonders of the enchanted castle.

Every night she sat down to dinner with the beast. He was quite fierce-looking, but his voice was quiet and gentle, and he always spoke kindly to Beauty. Soon she was no longer afraid of him and found herself growing more and more fond of him.

In fact Beauty came to look forward to their quiet evenings together.

After dinner they would walk through the beautiful gardens and talk of many things. No matter what they spoke of, the beast would ask Beauty the same question every night.

"Am I very ugly?" he asked her.

"Yes, you are," she would always answer, "but I like you anyway."

"Then will you marry me, Beauty?" he would ask.

"Oh, please do not ask me this question," she would say to the beast.

Beauty was happy in the magical castle, and she had grown very fond of the beast. But she missed her own home, her brothers and sisters, and her loving father.

One night in the garden she asked the beast to let her go home for a visit. He made her promise to come back in two months and gave her two magical trunks to fill with presents for her family. No matter how much she packed, the trunks were never full.

Then the beast gave her a ring with a large jewel in it and told her it would take her home and then bring her back. All she had to do was turn it on her finger, and she would be home the next day!

The next morning Beauty awoke to the sound of her father's voice! She was home in her own bed. Her family was very happy to see her. Her father's luck had finally returned, and his family was rich once more.

As the weeks passed, Beauty missed the beast's castle where she had been so happy. But most of all she missed the beast. She spent hours thinking of their long talks at dinnertime, and she fondly remembered their evening strolls through the beautiful gardens.

Beauty found that she was growing restless among her family, but she was afraid to tell them that she wanted to leave. She did not want to break her father's heart again.

One night she put the magic ring on her finger and looked into the jewel. There she saw the beast, lying in his garden. He seemed to be dying!

Beauty turned the ring on her finger and was magically returned to the enchanted garden. Suddenly she was by the side of the beast. He was so weak he could not speak. She lifted his head, and he opened his eyes to look at her one last time.

"Oh, please do not die!" cried Beauty. "I never knew it before, but I love you!"

At Beauty's words there was a sudden flash of light, and the beast leaped up. Beauty saw that her ugly friend had changed into a handsome prince! Beauty's love had freed the prince from a terrible spell. Since the two already loved each other, they were married and lived happily ever after in the enchanted castle.

LITTLE RED RIDING HOOD

Adapted by Jane Jerrard

Illustrated by Susan Spellman

Once upon a time, and it was a very long time ago, at the edge of a very large forest, there was a tiny village. At the end of the village, on the edge of the forest, lived a little girl and her mother.

The girl's grandmother loved her granddaughter more than kittens love mischief and had made her a beautiful red cloak with a hood. The little girl wore the velvet riding cloak everywhere she went. She wore it so often that the other villagers called her Little Red Riding Hood.

One day Little Red Riding Hood's mother asked her to take a basket of good food to her grandmother, who was feeling sick.

"Go quickly, dear, and don't wander through the forest," she told her little daughter. "Stay on the path. Grandmother is waiting." Little Red Riding Hood promised to go straight to her grandmother's. She put on her red cloak and set out right away.

Her grandmother's house was deep in the heart of the forest, but Little Red Riding Hood knew which path to take and was not afraid to walk alone. She was not even afraid when she met a wolf!

"Good morning," said the wolf.

"Good morning, wolf," said Little Red Riding Hood.

Now the wolf, as you probably know, was a wily animal and was not to be trusted. But he was very polite when he spoke to Little Red Riding Hood.

"Where are you going, little girl?" the wolf asked.

"To Grandmother's house," she said. "I am taking this basket of food to her because she is sick." She answered all his questions happily. She even told the wolf where her grandmother lived and how to get there!

While she chatted, the wily wolf was thinking about how much he would like to eat Little Red Riding Hood and her basket of food.

As the wolf walked with Little Red Riding Hood, he said, "You are marching along as if you were on your way to school! You should play awhile and pick some flowers!"

Little Red Riding Hood looked around her. She saw what a pretty day it was and thought the wolf was right. She should enjoy the morning and pick some wildflowers for her grandmother.

Little Red Riding Hood left the path and gathered the prettiest flowers she could find. She daydreamed a little as she searched, and she forgot about the promise she had made to her mother.

Meanwhile the wolf crept down the path until he was out of sight. Then he ran straight to Grandmother's house, lickety-split. Once he'd caught his breath, he knocked gently on the door.

"Who is it?" called Grandmother.

"It is Little Red Riding Hood. I've brought you some cake and bread and butter," said the wily wolf.

"Lift the latch and walk in," said Grandmother, for she was tucked in bed. But when she saw the wolf step in, she leaped right up, only to faint from fright!

The wolf, wanting only to eat Little Red Riding Hood, pushed the poor old woman under the bed. He disguised himself with her lacy cap and nightgown and jumped into her bed. There he waited.

When Little Red Riding Hood had picked an armload of perfect little wildflowers, she remembered her promise to her mother about her sick grandmother. She rushed to her grandmother's house and knocked on the door.

"Who is it?" called the wolf, who made his voice sound just like Little Red Riding Hood's grandmother.

"It is I, Little Red Riding Hood," called the girl.

"Lift the latch and walk in," said the wolf.

Little Red Riding Hood thought she could see her grandmother lying in bed, with her lacy cap pulled low and the covers tucked up to her chin.

The wolf said, "Come a bit closer, my dear," in a high, quavering voice. Little Red Riding Hood came right up to the bedside.

"My, Grandmother, what big ears you have!" she said, taking a step back.

"The better to hear you with, my dear," said the wolf.

"My, what big eyes you have, Grandmother!" called Little Red Riding Hood, taking another step back.

"The better to see you with, my dear."

"But, Grandmother, what big teeth you have!"

"The better to EAT you with!" cried the wolf.

With that the wolf leaped out of the bed and chased Little Red Riding Hood around the room! He was very hungry and had been looking forward to eating the little girl. But Little Red Riding Hood was too quick for the big, bad wolf. She jumped out of his reach and ran to the door.

Lucky for Little Red Riding Hood, the wolf was not used to wearing Grandmother's nightgown. He kept tripping and stumbling over the hem and had a hard time chasing Little Red Riding Hood.

Little Red Riding Hood ran straight out the open door. "Help! Help! a wolf!" cried Little Red Riding Hood.

It happened that a hunter, who had been after that wily wolf for days, was in the woods nearby. He had followed the wolf's footprints all the way up to the path to Grandmother's house.

When the hunter heard Little Red Riding Hood's cries for help, he raised his gun as quick as a wink and shot the wolf dead as he was leaping through the front door of her grandmother's house.

Little Red Riding Hood and the hunter went inside to find poor Grandmother rising to her feet, covered with dust from head to toe. Little Red Riding Hood ran to her arms for a comforting hug.

When she heard about their narrow escape from the wolf, Grandmother insisted on a party to thank the kind hunter. Little Red Riding Hood, Grandmother, and the hunter sat down at the kitchen table and shared the basket of good things to eat.

Forever after Little Red Riding Hood never left the path when she walked in the woods.

The GINGERBREAD MAN

Adapted by Carolyn Quattrocki

Illustrated by Tim Ellis

Once upon a time, a little old man was married to a little old woman, and they lived in a little old house. They never had any children, and they were very lonely. One day the little old woman said, "I will bake a gingerbread man. Then we will have a little boy to call our own."

The woman went into her kitchen and mixed flour, butter, milk, sugar, ginger, and cinnamon to make dough. Then she rolled it flat with her rolling pin.

She cut out the shape of a boy, gave him raisins for eyes, and a smiling mouth of pink frosting.

When the gingerbread was all baked, the old woman opened the oven door. To her surprise the gingerbread man jumped right out!

He hopped down from the baking pan and ran across the kitchen floor. He ran past the little old woman. Then he ran past the little old man and ran right out the front door of the little old house.

The little old man and the little old woman chased him out the door. They ran as fast as they could, but the gingerbread man ran faster. He looked over his shoulder, laughing and shouting,

Run, run, as fast as you can!
You can't catch me, I'm the gingerbread man!

And the old man and woman could not catch him.

The gingerbread man ran on and on until he met a cow. The cow said to him, "Stop, gingerbread man! I want to eat you!"

But the gingerbread man said, "I've run away from a little old woman and a little old man. And I can run away from you, I can!"

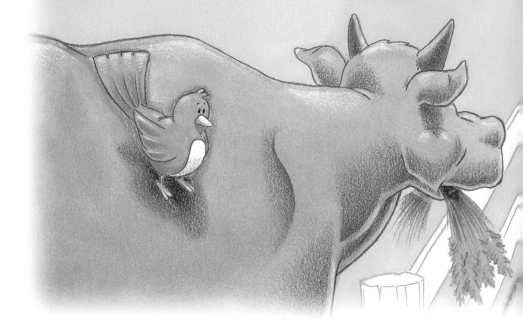

The gingerbread man ran faster and faster as the cow

began to chase him. As he ran, he looked over his shoulder,

laughing and shouting,

> *Run, run, as fast as you can!*
> *You can't catch me,*
> *I'm the gingerbread man!*

And the cow could not catch him.

The gingerbread man ran on until

he met a horse. "Stop, little boy," said the hungry horse.

"You look good enough to eat."

But the gingerbread man said, "I've run away from a

little old woman, a little old man, and a cow. And I can

run away from you, I can!"

As the horse began to chase him, the gingerbread man ran faster and faster. He looked over his shoulder, laughing and shouting,

Run, run, as fast as you can!
You can't catch me,
I'm the gingerbread man!

And the horse could not catch him.

The gingerbread man ran on and on until he came to some farmers working in a field. "Stop, little boy," they said. "We want to eat you."

The gingerbread man said, "I've run away from a little old woman, a little old man, a cow, and a horse. And I can run away from you, I can!"

As the farmers chased him, the gingerbread man ran faster and faster. He looked over his shoulder, laughing and shouting,

Run, run, as fast as you can!
You can't catch me,
I'm the gingerbread man!

And the farmers could not catch him.

The gingerbread man ran on and on until he came to a small village. All the people of the village watched as the little gingerbread man ran through their streets. Even though nobody in the village chased him, the gingerbread man shouted at them as he ran through town.

He said, "I've run away from a little old woman, a little old man, a cow, a horse, and three farmers. And I can run away from you, I can!"

As the people watched, the gingerbread man laughed and shouted,

Run, run, as fast as you can!
You can't catch me,
I'm the gingerbread man!

Over the next hill, the gingerbread man ran past a fox.
This clever old fox also wanted to eat the gingerbread man,
but he was too sly to say so. Instead the fox said, "I'll just
run along with you, wherever you're going."

But again the gingerbread man ran faster and faster.
He called, "I've run away from a little old woman, a little

old man, a cow, a horse, and three farmers. And I can run away from you, I can!"

The gingerbread man laughed and shouted,

> Run, run, as fast as you can!
> You can't catch me,
> I'm the gingerbread man!

Soon the gingerbread man came to a river. He knew
he could never swim across the wide river, but he wanted
to keep running away from the little old man and the little
old woman and the cow and the horse and the farmers who
were all chasing him.

The fox said, "Just jump on my tail, and I'll take you across the river." He jumped on the fox's tail, and the fox swam into the water just as the little old man and the little old woman and the cow and the horse and the three farmers reached the bank of the river.

Once they were in the river, the fox said, "You'd better move to my back, or you might fall off in this deep water."

A little farther on, the fox said, "You might get wet, so you'd better come sit on my shoulder." The gingerbread man sat on the fox's shoulder.

When they were almost to the other side of the river, the fox said to the gingerbread man, "This is the deepest water yet. You had better climb onto my head." So then the gingerbread man climbed from the fox's shoulder onto his head.

Finally the fox said, "I'm getting tired. Would you please jump onto my nose?"

As soon as they reached shore, SNAP! The fox ate the gingerbread man in one bite.

After all gingerbread men are meant to be eaten. That is what they are for!